For Isabel and Miranda, whose mother, Janetta,
had the idea for this book ~ *M.H.*

For Andrea ~ *J.O.*

A Twist in the Tail
Animal Stories from Around the World

Mary Hoffman

Illustrated by Jan Ormerod

HENRY HOLT AND COMPANY • NEW YORK

Henry Holt and Company, Inc.
Publishers since 1866
115 West 18th Street
New York, New York 10011

Henry Holt is a registered trademark of Henry Holt and Company, Inc.

First published in the United States in 1998 by
Henry Holt and Company, Inc.
Published in Canada by Fitzhenry & Whiteside Ltd.,
195 Allstate Parkway, Markham, Ontario L3R 4T8.
A Twist in the Tail was edited, designed, and produced by Frances Lincoln Limited,
4 Torriano Mews, Torriano Avenue, London NW5 2RZ.

Library of Congress Catalog Card Number: 97-78068

ISBN 0-8050-5946-6
First American edition—1998

Printed in Hong Kong

1 3 5 7 9 10 8 6 4 2

Contents

A Birthday Surprise

Anancy was a spider, and a very tricksy one too. But sometimes he was a man—he could change whenever he wanted.

Anancy had a birthday coming up. His wife decided to throw a surprise party for him and invited Tiger, Dog, Monkey, and Goat.

Although the animals loved parties, they weren't at all sure about accepting. Anancy was famous for taking other people's food.

"Perhaps it's a trick," said Goat.

"Perhaps it's not really his birthday at all," said Dog.

"Perhaps the surprise will be on us," said Monkey.

"Perhaps there will be chocolate cake," said Tiger.

That made up their minds for them—they all loved chocolate cake. But they couldn't decide what to get Anancy for a present.

"Gloves?" suggested Goat.

"We'd have to buy four pairs," said Dog.

"Shoes?" said Monkey.

"Same problem," said Tiger.

In the end, they settled on a plump white chicken for Anancy to keep in his backyard.

"That way he won't keep stealing ours," they said.

They put the chicken in a basket and set out for Anancy's house.

But on the way a terrible wind sprang up and blew the chicken out of the basket, up in the air, into the next village, and down into Mr. Man's cooking pot.

Now the animals didn't have a present. When they arrived at Anancy's house and he saw the empty basket, he flew into a big tantrum and the animals fled.

"Is this the surprise?" he screamed, stamping all his eight feet. "An empty basket? Go away. No cake for you!"

Anancy sat at the table. He put on his party hat and blew his party whistle. He tied a red balloon to his chair. His wife sang "Happy Birthday" to him.

"Shall I cut the cake?" she asked.

"No," said Anancy, sadly. "It's no fun eating cake on your own. Perhaps they were just getting their own back for all the tricks I've played on them."

And he sent a message to the animals by carrier pigeon. It said:

Please come back and help me eat my cake.
Anancy.
P.S. No more tricks!

"Good," said Tiger. "He's going to give up his tricks. Let's go."

But the Wind, who had taken the chicken, peeked in at Anancy's window and saw him looking sad on his birthday. Wind felt sorry for him. So as the animals made their way back to Anancy's party, Wind curled around a tree and shook it till a big coconut fell into the basket.

Next, Wind plucked a bunch of flowers from a field and blew them into the basket. Then he scooped up two speckled brown eggs from the chicken coop and dropped them in the basket. And finally, Wind startled a peacock and made it drop two beautiful tail feathers, which he whisked away into the basket.

So when they arrived, the four friends were laden with presents for the birthday spider.

"Ooh," squealed Anancy. "Presents!"

He cracked open the coconut and drank the milk. He put the flowers in a vase and the eggs in his larder. And he stuck the two peacock feathers in his party hat and strutted around the room on his eight hairy legs, very pleased with himself.

The four friends ate as much cake as they possibly could. And Mr. Man's family ate as much chicken stew as *they* could.

It was a day of surprise treats all round!

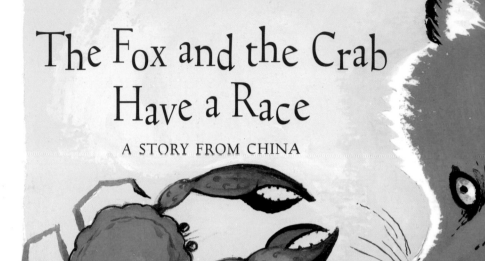

The Fox and the Crab Have a Race

A STORY FROM CHINA

Fox was very proud of his running. He thought he was the fastest thing on four legs. And he didn't think much of anyone who was slower than him.

"What a crawler you are!" he said one day to Crab. "Don't you ever run anywhere?"

"Yes," said Crab. "I run from the river-mud to the bank, and back again."

"Pooh!" said Fox. "That's not far. Look at all your legs and feet. If I had as many as you, I would run even faster than I do. As it is, you, even with all those legs, are so much slower than me that you must be very silly indeed."

Crab thought for a bit, then asked, "Would you like to run a race with me then, Fox? Since I am so slow and silly, you are bound to win."

Now Fox was so proud and so rude that he couldn't resist a chance to show off, even though the race would be so unfair. So he agreed.

"But, Fox," said Crab, "you have another advantage over me. You hold your big bushy tail up as you run. Perhaps it catches the wind in it. If you would allow me to weigh it down with something, we would be more equal."

"Equal?" sneered the proud Fox. "That'll be the day! But you can tie down my tail if you want."

"Just let me fasten something on to your tail," said Crab, "and when I call 'READY,' you start to run."

"All right," said Fox.

Soon Fox felt a weight on his tail and Crab called "READY." Fox loped off as fast as he could go. But Crab had grabbed Fox's tail in his big pincers! He clung on as hard as he could and, however fast Fox ran, Crab was right behind him.

Soon Fox began to tire. He stopped, panting, and looked around for Crab. Imagine his astonishment when he saw Crab right beside him, waving a claw at him.

"Hello, Fox," said Crab. "I thought you were going to outrun me easily. But here we are, neck and neck."

Fox felt very foolish. He slunk away with his beautiful tail between his legs. He didn't realize how he had been tricked. But after his race with Crab, he never boasted about his running, though I'm afraid he never really learned to be polite.

The Bright Blue Jackal

A STORY FROM INDIA

There was once a jackal who lived with his family in a forest in India. He was more inquisitive than his brothers and sisters, and it often got him into trouble.

One day, he wandered near a town at the edge of the forest and saw a tub full of something outside a house. He climbed up to take a look, sniffed, stretched to see better . . . and fell in. Now, the house belonged to a tailor and the tub was full of dye, a bright blue color called indigo, for dyeing *saris* and *cholis* and *shalwar kameez.*

Jackal splashed around in the dye, but the sides of the tub were too steep for him to climb out. Suddenly he heard someone coming, so he decided to play dead.

"What's this?" said the tailor crossly. "A jackal drowned in my best indigo dye? What a waste of a lovely color!" And he tipped poor Jackal out of the tub. Straight away, dead Jackal became live Jackal, and ran away back into the forest. The tailor scratched his head. Why should a jackal play dead in his dye tub? He never found out.

But Jackal, safe in the forest, was looking at himself in a pool. He saw a bright blue jackal's face. And when he looked over his shoulder, he saw a bright blue jackal's tail. And when he held up his front leg, he saw a bright blue jackal's paw, with bright blue toenails.

"What a handsome fellow I am!" he cried. "Surely this will bring me luck. Now, how can I make the best use of my lovely blue coat?"

It wasn't long before he met up with the rest of his pack, who scarcely recognized him.

"Brother?" they said. "Is that you? What happened?"

"Something very important," said Blue Jackal. "I was chosen by the Goddess of this forest to be king here. She changed my color to show that I am different. From now on, you must obey me."

Well, the other jackals had to admit he was different. No one had ever seen a blue jackal before. They supposed they had better do as he said.

But Blue Jackal wasn't content with bossing his family around. He called all the other animals of the forest together and told them he was a completely new kind of animal. From now on, all the animals must treat him as their king.

The tigers and lions believed him. The monkeys and mongooses believed him. The snakes and the rats, the hares and the turtles, the hawks and owls and mice all

believed him. And they treated Blue Jackal as a king, never realizing that he was just an ordinary jackal dyed blue.

Blue Jackal became terribly spoiled. He never had to hunt for food, because the lions and tigers brought it to him. He never had to wash, because the monkeys groomed him. He slept on a bed of soft leaves and blossoms. He expected all the other animals to bow down before him. He became unbearable.

"He has gone too far," said the other jackals. "Blue he may be, but he's still only a jackal. If the other animals knew that, they wouldn't give any more respect to him than they do to us."

So they plotted against Blue Jackal. They waited till the first stars were appearing in the sky, then crept close to where King Jackal was holding court, wreathed in garlands of flowers. The birds of the forest were singing a concert for him. The monkeys were fanning him with leaves. The lions and tigers were standing guard over him.

Then the moon rose in the clear night sky and the oldest jackal threw back his head and began to howl. All the others joined in. Blue Jackal heard the sound and the hairs on his back rose up. Deep inside him, he was just a jackal and he couldn't resist the age-old habit of howling at the moon.

"Ah-oooooohhh!" howled Blue Jackal, throwing back his head and tossing off his garlands.

"What is that racket?" growled the lions and tigers. "Listen! The king is nothing but a common jackal."

"A jackal, a jackal!" screeched the monkeys, dropping their fans. "After him!"

For Blue Jackal, realizing that his career as a king was over, had very sensibly run away. All the animals gave chase, but they couldn't catch him. Blue Jackal was never seen in the forest again. And I'm sure this story must be true, because I never have heard of a blue jackal in the forests of India. Have you?

The Wolf Who Loved Sheep
A LOS NOBOS STORY FROM CAPE VERDE

Los Nobos was very fond of sheep. He would climb up onto the rocks and look down on the sheep nibbling the grass below, smiling at them with his big wide mouth and strong white teeth.

"Oh, I do love sheep," he said to himself. "Any kind of sheep. But I like the fattest ones best."

Los Nobos' favorite sheep was called Bagatta. She was the plumpest sheep in the flock and he watched her most often. Bagatta was rather a vain sheep and she was flattered by his attention.

"I expect Los Nobos is looking at me because I am so beautiful," said Bagatta. She started making sheep's eyes at him. Los Nobos came down off the rocks to talk to her.

"I can always eat you tomorrow, I suppose," he said. "We'll wait here till it gets dark, and then you can show me the cheese."

Soon it was dark and a full moon rose in the sky. Bagatta led Los Nobos to the lake and showed him the big golden round cheese. In dived the wolf, but somehow he could not get the cheese in his mouth, however close he got. As soon as he snapped his jaws, it dissolved into a thousand gold waterdrops. He tried and tried till he was exhausted.

Los Nobos crawled out of the water, dripping and panting. He asked a passing bird about the cheese.

"That's the moon, you noodle," said the bird. "You've been trying to eat its reflection."

"Grrrr!" said Los Nobos. "That sheep has tricked me again!" He shook himself and bounded after Bagatta.

"That was no cheese!" he growled. "It was the moon's reflection!"

"Oh, I'm so sorry, Los Nobos," bleated Bagatta. "You must forgive me. I'm only a silly sheep."

"Forgive you?" said Los Nobos. "You've tricked me twice, and now I'm going to EAT you!"

He opened his big red mouth wide enough to eat a whole sheep and pointed at it with his hairy paw.

"Very well," said Bagatta, though she was shaking in her woolly fleece. "I can see I am going to be your dinner and I hope you enjoy your meal. But just let me ask one favor."

"Favor?" said Los Nobos. "After all your tricks?"

"What do you want?" asked Bagatta.

"Nothing," said Los Nobos. "Just to talk to you. I love sheep, you know." *Especially plump ones,* he added under his breath.

"Do you want my autograph?" asked Bagatta.

"NO!" said Los Nobos. "I want you for DINNER!" And he prepared to jump on the silly sheep.

Danger sharpened Bagatta's wits. She saw at once how foolish she had been to let a wolf flatter her.

"It would be an honor to be your dinner, Los Nobos," she said. "But I am hardly good enough to make you a meal as I am. Let me eat all the juiciest grass and fatten myself up. Come back in a month, and then I'll be a really tasty dish."

"Very well," said Los Nobos, and he went away, laughing at how stupid Bagatta was.

A month later, he came looking for her and found her lying on her back in the rocks, with her feet braced against the biggest one.

"Am I glad to see you, Los Nobos!" gasped Bagatta. "This rock was about to fall and roll down onto the farmer's house. If it did, the farmer would be squashed and all his sheep sold. So far, I've been able to stop it rolling down, but my legs are getting tired. Will you take over from me for a while?"

The flock all sold! What a terrible idea! If that happened, there would be no more sheep for Los Nobos. So he carefully slid in beside Bagatta and braced his legs against the big rock.

"Thank you," called Bagatta, as she skipped down the hill. "I will come back as soon as I have rested."

Los Nobos lay upside down under the rock for two days, waiting for Bagatta to return. Then he simply had to stretch his legs and crawled out from under the rock. Nothing happened. The rock stayed exactly where it was. Los Nobos realized he had been tricked. He bounded off down the rocks, hungrier than ever.

He found Bagatta and cornered her with a snarl.

"Dinnertime!" he growled.

Bagatta's heart was pounding, but she kept cool.

"Oh dear, what a shame," she said. "If you eat me now, you'll have no room for the lovely big round cheese that will be floating in the lake tonight."

Los Nobos was so hungry that he didn't like the idea of missing out on the cheese.

"Yes," said Bagatta. "Please swallow me whole. I hate the idea of being chewed into bits."

Los Nobos didn't mind. The sooner he had that plump sheep in his tummy, the better.

"All right," he said, opening his mouth a bit wider.

"Close your eyes and stand back," said Bagatta. "I'll run straight into your mouth."

Los Nobos closed his eyes. The next minute he was choking and coughing and spitting. Bagatta had stuffed a whole heap of prickly plants into Los Nobos' mouth.

"Oh, Bagatta, you taste terrible!" howled Los Nobos, as he ran back to the lake to cool his burning mouth. "I would rather go hungry than eat you."

And he never tried to eat Bagatta again. As for Bagatta, she never again made the mistake of making sheep's eyes at a wolf.

The Magpie and the Milk

A STORY FROM TURKEY

An old woman was milking her cow. She left the pail in the yard while she went to fetch wood for her fire.

"I'll boil that milk," she thought, "and have a nice hot drink."

But while she was away collecting firewood, a handsome magpie flew over the yard and spotted the milk-pail. "Lovely," thought the magpie. "Fresh creamy milk. What a treat!" He flew down and perched on the edge of the pail. But the magpie made rather an awkward landing and, instead of just dipping his beak in, he lost his balance, scrabbled to keep his footing, and, oh dear, only succeeded in tipping the pail right over.

Magpie was still shaking milk off his feathers and catching the drops in his beak when the old woman came back with her pile of firewood. Straight away she realized what had happened and made a grab for the thief. Magpie squawked and struggled so hard to get away that he left his handsome blue-black tail in the old woman's hand.

"Old woman, old woman!" he chittered. "Give me back my tail!"

"Certainly," said the old woman. "Just as soon as you fetch me some more milk."

So Magpie went to the cowshed and said, "Cow, cow, give me some milk. Then I can give it to the old woman and she will give me back my tail."

"Certainly," said the cow. "Just as soon as you fetch me some nice juicy grass."

Magpie hopped away—for he couldn't fly properly without his tail to balance him—to the nearest field.

"Field, field," he said, "give me some of your green juicy grass. Then I can give it to the cow and she will give me some milk. Then I can give the milk to the old woman and she will give me back my tail."

"Certainly," said the field. "Just as soon as you fetch me some cool refreshing water."

Magpie hopped off down the road to look for the water-carrier. When he found him, the bird said, "Water-carrier, water-carrier, please give me some cool water for the field. Then the field will give me some juicy grass, I can give the grass to the cow, the cow will give me some milk, I will give the milk to the old woman, and she will give me back my tail."

"Certainly," said the water-carrier. "Just as soon as you bring me a freshly laid egg for my lunch."

So the tired magpie hopped off to find a hen. "Hen, hen," he gasped, when he found her. "Please, will you lay me an egg? Then I can give it to the water-carrier and he will give me some cool water and I can give the water to the field and the field will give me some nice juicy grass and I shall give the grass to the cow and the cow will give me some milk and I can give it to the old woman and…she…will…give…me…back…my…tail." He sank, exhausted, into the dust.

"Gracious me," said the hen. "Is that really you, Magpie? What a state you are in, with your glossy feathers all dusty and your beautiful tail gone! Well, when all's said and done, we are both birds and we should help one another." She settled down, and after a minute started to cluck. "There you are, Magpie, a nice fresh egg."

"Oh, thank you, thank you, dear hen," said Magpie. He shook his feathers and carefully rolled the egg back to the water-carrier.

Then the water-carrier gave the water to Magpie…

Magpie gave the water to the field…

The field gave the grass to Magpie…

Magpie gave the grass to the cow…

The cow gave the milk—quick, fetch the bucket—

to Magpie…

and Magpie gave the milk to the old woman.

"Now can I have my tail back?" he said. And the old woman gave him back his beautiful blue-black tail feathers.

All around the yard flew the happy magpie, flaunting his tail and singing his tuneless song. And the old woman set her saucepan of milk on the fire and settled down to enjoy a nice hot drink

The Pelican and the Fish

A STORY FROM MALAYSIA

Once there was a fish who lived with his wife and little ones in a freshwater pool at the bottom of a foaming waterfall. He had a happy, peaceful life with no worries.

Then one day the fish heard some bad news. A pelican came and stood on his tall thin legs at the edge of the pool. "Oh dear," he said. "What a pretty pool. Isn't it a shame that it's going to dry up!"

"Dry up?" said Fish, his fins quivering. "What do you mean?"

"Haven't you heard?" said Pelican. "There's a drought. All the rivers are running dry. Soon this lovely waterfall will stop pouring its waters into the pool and then the pool will dry up in the sun."

"But what am I to do?" said Fish. "What about my family—my wife and all our little ones?"

Pelican said nothing, but his eyes lit up greedily when Fish mentioned his many babies. "What am I to do?" Fish repeated. "We *must* find a new home."

"Well, there I may be able to help," said Pelican. "I have seen more of the world than you have, flying around as I do. And I happen to know of another pool, which is fed by an underground stream. That pool will never dry up."

"Wonderful!" said Fish. "But how can we get there?"

"Easy," said Pelican. "I can carry you there in my big beak and you can have a look round. Then, if you like the pool, I could come back for the rest of your family."

Fish thought this was a fine offer. Pelican lowered his big baggy beak into the water and opened it so that Fish could swim in. It was dark in there, and Fish was very uncomfortable. Then Pelican walked downstream a little way to another pool and let Fish out into the water. But Fish thought he had traveled miles.

"Oh, what a lovely pool!" said Fish. "We'll be very happy here. How can we ever thank you?"

Pelican smiled to himself.

Fish swam around in his new pool waiting for his family to join him. He waited and waited, but they didn't come. Fish began to worry.

Meanwhile, back at the first pool, Fish's wife and children were eager to get into Pelican's beak for their journey. But when Pelican had scooped them up in his beak, he took them around the corner…and swallowed them! Afterwards he still felt hungry, so he went back to the pool to look for something more.

Pelican found Crab sitting in the pool, waving his claws.

"Oh dear," said Pelican. "Isn't it a shame that this pool is drying up?"

But Crab was wiser and cleverer than Fish. He had seen everything that had happened, and he thought that Pelican shouldn't get away with it.

"Come nearer and tell me all about it," said Crab.

Pelican bent down—and at once Crab grabbed his neck with his big pincers and squeezed hard. Out came the little fishes, one by one.

Crab squeezed again, and out came Fish's wife.

Crab squeezed once more to try to rescue Fish, but of course Fish himself was not in Pelican's pouch. So Crab let go, and Pelican staggered off to try his tricks in another pool.

After waiting another whole day, Fish swam upstream and found his first home still there. The waterfall was splashing down as fast and clear as ever. And best of all, his wife and children were swimming around happily.

Fish was glad that he had seen the world, but he was even more glad to be home!

The Fox and the Boastful Brave

AN IROQUOIS STORY FROM NORTH AMERICA

One fine day, a hungry fox was walking down the road. His tummy was rumbling so loudly that he almost didn't hear the sound of someone coming. Just in time, he heard someone singing. Fox dashed off the path and hid behind a bush.

Over the crest of the hill he saw a tall feather. Fox crouched down and prepared to pounce on the bird. Imagine his surprise when he saw that the "bird" was riding a horse! The feather was an ornament stuck in the headdress of a handsome young brave who was riding along the path, singing as he went, "No one is braver than Heron Feather. No one is handsomer than Heron Feather. No one is a better fisherman than Heron Feather. And I should know, for I am he."

Fox didn't care if the man was brave or handsome, but he pricked up his ears at the word "fisherman," for where there are fishermen, there are fish. And a tasty fish would just suit Fox. His nose twitched. A delightful fishy smell was coming out of the brave's leather bag.

Heron Feather continued his boastful song. He was on his way to ask a young woman called Swaying Reed to marry him, and he was making himself feel bolder by singing his own praises.

"No one is wiser than Heron Feather. No one is kinder than Heron Feather. No one has finer clothes than Heron Feather. And I should know, for I am he."

Fox bounded ahead of the brave and lay down on the path, playing dead. Soon he heard the sound of hoofbeats and singing.

"No one is stronger than…what's this? A dead fox? When Swaying Reed's mother sees this, she will know what a great hunter I am. A fox is bound to impress her, even though it's such a skinny specimen."

And he picked Fox up, flung him into his bag of fish and laced it shut again. Heron Feather remounted and began a new song.

"No one is a greater hunter than Heron Feather…"

Inside the bag, surrounded by lovely smelly fish, Fox's mouth was watering. He waited a few minutes, then gnawed a big hole in the side of the bag. One by one, all the fish fell out, followed last of all by Fox. Heron Feather was singing too loudly to notice.

Fox made his way slowly back along the path, stopping to eat each fish as he went. "Skinny specimen, indeed!" he said, licking his lips. His tummy was fuller than it had been for days.

Meanwhile, Heron Feather had arrived at Swaying Reed's lodge. He stopped his horse outside and sang

his boasting song about how clever, handsome, and brave he was, what a great hunter and what a great fisherman. (In fact, he hadn't caught those fish at all. He had traded his mother's beaded moccasins for them.)

All Swaying Reed's neighbors gathered around to admire her bold boyfriend. Heron Feather reached for his bag of fish to show Swaying Reed and her mother what a good husband and provider he would be.

When he saw it was empty, with a large hole in it, he stopped in mid-song.

He sang no more, but turned his horse and rode away, back to his own lodge. Behind him, he heard Swaying Reed's neighbors singing a new song.

"No one is a bigger liar than Heron Feather. No one is a bigger boaster than Heron Feather. No one is a bigger fool than Heron Feather. And you should know, for you are he!"

Back in his den, Fox burped contentedly. "It is one thing to catch a fox," he said, "but quite another to keep it."

The Tortoise Who Rode
an Elephant

A YORUBA STORY FROM NIGERIA

Tortoise was a boaster and a bragger. He had to be better than anyone else and he didn't mind what tricks he played to prove it.

One day, Tortoise boasted that he was going to ride into town on Elephant. All the animals laughed and jeered at him.

"Why should mighty Elephant let a little pie-on-legs like you ride on his back?" they mocked.

Well, that made Tortoise mad. "I bet you a pot of gold that I will ride into town on Elephant!" he insisted. Then he crawled off into the forest to Elephant's favorite pool.

"Good morning, Tortoise," trumpeted Elephant. "What's the news?"

"Oh, just the usual silly gossip," said Tortoise. "Nothing for a powerful animal like you to worry about."

"What gossip?" said Elephant, suspiciously. "Tell me."

"Well," said Tortoise, pretending he didn't want to say, "everyone is saying you never come into town. Of course I said you were far too busy and important to bother with such things but…"

"Go on," said Elephant.

"…they said—forgive me for repeating it—that you are…too fat and lazy to walk all the way to town."

Elephant snorted and trumpeted, and pulled up a nearby tree.

Tortoise hastily hid his head and feet inside his shell, waiting for Elephant to get over his fit of temper.

"Fat and lazy, am I?" roared Elephant.

"Not at all, Elephant," said Tortoise. "Why don't you show them all you're not, by walking into town now? I could be your guide."

So the two animals set off together, big and small. But it's not always the biggest who come out best where tricks are concerned.

After a while, Tortoise called out to Elephant, "Wait, wait. I can't keep up with you. You're going too fast."

"We'll never get to town this week if we go at your pace," grumbled Elephant.

"Then let me travel on your back, mighty one," said Tortoise. "I'll be able to see where we're going, and you can get along faster."

So Elephant curled his great trunk around Tortoise and lifted him up onto his broad back. Tortoise rode into town like a king.

When all the other animals saw Elephant coming, they couldn't believe their eyes. Tortoise really was riding him! Even though they had lost their bet, they couldn't help laughing at the ridiculous sight.

The noise of their laughter made Elephant panic.

He charged around, knocking over market stalls and bumping into houses. Tortoise clung to his back for dear life. But finally, Elephant realized that the animals were laughing at him.

"Why are they laughing at me?" he demanded.

Tortoise was such a boaster, he couldn't keep it to himself. "They are laughing because I am riding you into town as if I were your master and you my servant. What's more, I bet them I could do it, and now I'm going to be rich!"

Elephant harrumphed and trumpeted, and flung Tortoise off his back into a muddy swamp. Then he lowered his trunk into the swamp and sprayed dirty water all over the other animals, until they ran away. Elephant stormed off into the forest and never came back to town again.

But Tortoise didn't mind a bit. He swam through the muddy swamp and out onto the land. Then he crawled off to the marketplace and collected his gold.

As long as he had something to boast about, Tortoise was always perfectly happy.

The Very Clever Rabbit

Once upon a time there was a very clever rabbit, who owned a nice little farm. Her best friend was a beautiful parrot with lovely red and green wings and a blue tail. They were both rather lazy. Rabbit didn't like all the work it took to dig the land and plant the crops and keep them watered, and all the trouble it was to harvest them and take them to market. And Parrot didn't like the way the farm took up all his friend's time so that she was never able to play.

So Rabbit decided to sell her farm. First she asked the plump brown hen, "Would you like to buy my little farm?"

"You can have it for a hundred *pesos*," added Parrot.

"A hundred *pesos*?" thought the plump brown hen. "That's not much!" So she said yes.

"Give me the money now," said Rabbit, "and you can have the farm on the day of the harvest."

So they made a deal.

But later that day, the two friends also sold the farm to
a smart red fox, a sandy dog, a glossy spotted jaguar, and
even a man. And they made the same deal every time.
    Rabbit and Parrot counted their money and went to sleep.

On the morning of the harvest, Rabbit got up very early and picked all the corn, while Parrot sat in the highest branch of the tree, keeping watch. Soon he saw the plump brown hen waddling along the road.

"Quarter to ten, here comes the hen," he called out to Rabbit.

"I've come for my farm," said the plump brown hen.

"Of course," said Rabbit. "Sit down and have some nice cold lemonade. Perhaps you'd like a little of this fine corn to peck at?"

But Parrot had seen the smart red fox slinking along the road.

"Look out! Look out! The fox is about!" he screeched.

"Quick," said Rabbit to the plump brown hen. "Hide inside the corn basket!" And she did.

"I've come for my farm," said the fox.

"Of course," said Rabbit. "Sit down and have some cold lemonade. And I have a nice plump hen somewhere…"

But just then, Parrot spotted the sandy dog loping down the road.

"Sound the alarm! There's a dog on the farm!" he squawked.

"Quick," said Rabbit. "Hide under this blanket. I'll get rid of him."

"I've come for my farm," said the dog, his nose twitching.

"Of course," said Rabbit. "Sit down and have some nice cold lemonade. And perhaps you could help me with a problem. I think we have a fox on the farm…"

Just then, Parrot spied the glossy spotted jaguar stalking down the road.

"Oh, my hat!" he cried. "The great spotted cat!"

"Quick," said Rabbit to the sandy dog. "You'd better hide behind my rocking-chair or the jaguar will see you." And he did.

"I've come for my farm," said the jaguar, sniffing the air. "And I haven't had any breakfast!"

"Have some nice cold lemonade," said Rabbit nervously, "and perhaps I can find you someone, I mean something, to eat."

From high in the tree, Parrot could see the man striding along the road to the farm.

"Oh, this isn't fun!" he shrieked, flying down onto the porch. "It's a man…with a gun!"

"Quick," said Rabbit to the trembling jaguar. "Jump in my hammock. The man won't notice you there." And she did.

"I've come for my farm," said the man.

"Of course," squeaked Rabbit. "Sit down and have some cold lemonade."

But just then, the hen finished all the corn in the basket and came fluttering out to look for more. The fox leapt out from under the blanket and chased her down the road. The dog jumped out from behind the rocking-chair and ran after the fox. The hungry jaguar burst out of the hammock with a growl and bounded after the dog. And the man hurled himself off the porch and rushed after the disappearing jaguar, waving his gun.

Soon all was peaceful and quiet on the farm. The clever rabbit and the beautiful parrot sipped their lemonade on the porch.

"It's funny how no one wanted the farm after all," said Rabbit, arranging her money in neat piles.

"Hmm," said Parrot, stretching his beautiful wings. "It's amazing how some folks just can't make up their minds."

"Never mind," said Rabbit, "at least I got the harvest in." They both laughed. "Now we can play," said Parrot. And they did.

The Animal Who Couldn't Make Up Its Mind

A CREATION STORY FROM AUSTRALIA

At the beginning of the world, the animals didn't have their present shapes. They hid in the darkness of caves, some in the shape of dim shadows, some in the form of blocks of ice, others already wearing fur or feathers but looking quite different from the way they do today.

This was before Yhi, the sun goddess, opened her bright eyes and filled the world with warmth and light. She entered the dark caves and turned the misty shapes into a throng of flying insects. She thawed the blocks of ice and out of them came all the fish and snakes and reptiles.

She coaxed the other animals out into the sunlight and they all loved her.

But Yhi was not going to stay on the earth; she was going back up into the heavens to shine for all the world.

When Yhi said she was going back to the sky, the animals were all very sad. When the first night fell and the darkness came back, they all cried. How excited and happy they were the next morning when they saw Yhi again sailing through the sky, shedding her golden light all over the world!

For a while, the animals were content to be the way they were. Then they started wanting a change. The animals who lived in water wanted to be on the dry land. The land-dwellers wanted to see what it was like in the sky, and the ones who could fly wanted to swim instead. They began to mope and hide away.

Yhi looked down from the sky and saw not a single animal. Even the plants, which had sprung to life in Yhi's path wherever her feet touched the ground, had begun to wilt. Yhi was worried, and she came down to earth one last time. The animals saw her coming, surrounded by a golden glow. They streamed toward her from all over the land.

"Yhi has come back!" they cried. "Surely she will listen to what we want."

They explained their wishes and Yhi listened to them.

"I should like to be able to wriggle into shady places and hide," said Wombat.

"I want big strong legs and a tail," said Kangaroo.

"Wings for me," said Bat. "I want to fly."

"And I want legs," said Lizard. "I'm tired of squirming along on my tummy."

One by one they came—Koala and Mopoke and Pelican and Stick Insect and Frog—and chose their new forms. Yhi was sad, because she knew that if she changed the creatures, they could never go back to being the way they were before. But she gave them all their wishes and sent them away, knowing that their lives were going to be changed forever.

She was turning away, getting ready to return to the sky, when she noticed one last, shy, quiet animal.

"What about you?" she asked gently. "How would you like to be different?"

"Um," said the animal, "I *think* I'd like to have fur to keep me warm in the water."

"Very well," said Yhi. "I did that for Water-rat." And she gave the animal fur.

"Oh, did you?" said the little animal. "Maybe I should have something different. A hard, round-ended bill would be useful for finding food on the river bed."

"I did that for Duck," said Yhi. And she gave the animal a bill.

"Duck, eh?" said the little animal. "Well, what else can I have? Claws perhaps, like Dingo's, to defend myself and dig a shelter in the river bank."

"Claws you shall have," said Yhi. And she gave the animal claws.

"Do I look like Dingo?" asked the animal.

"Not really," said Yhi.

"Like Duck?"

"Not completely."

"Like Water-rat, then?"

"Not exactly," said the sun goddess, laughing. She bent down and picked the strange-looking animal up in her arms.

"You don't look like any of the other animals," she said. "I shall call you Platypus."

And Platypus scuttled away back to his river, well-pleased with his new shape and new name.

When the first visitors to Australia came from other countries, they thought all the animals were very strange. They looked at them and thought that someone must have played tricks on them to make them the way they were. And most of all, they laughed when they saw Platypus. They thought he must be a joke. But every animal in

Australia chose its own shape, even Platypus, who wasn't quite sure whether he wanted to be a bird or a mammal or a fish. So he ended up completely different from everyone else!

About the Stories

Many of these animal stories contain a trick, a surprise, or both.
Often this means that a smaller or weaker animal outsmarts a bigger,
stronger one, or even a human being. Not surprisingly, a lot of these
twists and tricks are connected with where the next meal is coming from!

A Birthday Surprise

This is an Anancy story from the Caribbean. Anancy the Spiderman traveled from Ghana to the Caribbean in the memories of the slaves who survived the journey. He is a trickster, but here he thinks a trick is being played on him.

Source: Adapted from the Internet http://www.ucalgary.ca/~dkbrown/storfolk.html, section Folktales from around the World.

The Fox and the Crab Have a Race

A variant on the Hare and Tortoise story in *Aesop's Fables*. This version is from China, but I've found it in other cultures too.

Source: Adapted from *Chinese Fables and Folk Stories* by Mary Hayes Davis and Chow-Leung (American Book Co., 1908).

The Bright Blue Jackal

This Indian story has a touch of "The Emperor's New Clothes" about it: when the animals see through Jackal's bluff, they drive him out.

Source: Retold from the Internet http://www.ece.ucdavis.edu/~darsie/tales.html, in a version by Amy Friedman. The original story is found in the *Hitopadesha*, a collection of Indian fables.

The Wolf Who Loved Sheep

In this story from Cape Verde, an island off the coast of West Africa, the "silly" sheep manages to deceive the wolf.

Source: Retold from the Internet http://www.ucalgary.ca/~dkbrown/storfolk.html, section Folktales from around the World.

The Magpie and the Milk

This is a Turkish variant on the cumulative story that many people in Britain know as "The Old Woman and Her Pig."

Source: Retold from *A Treasury of Turkish Folk-Tales for Children* by Barbara K. Walker © 1988 (North Haven, Conn.: Linnet Books/London: Oxford University Press).

The Pelican and the Fish

A story from the Malay Peninsula, found in other versions in other parts of the world.

SOURCE: Adapted from "The Deceitful Pelican" in *Folktales and Fables of the World* by Barbara Hayes (David Bateman Ltd., Australia, 1987).

The Fox and the Boastful Brave

An Iroquois story, in which, unlike the Crab story, Fox wins. Here it is the man who is boastful and gets taken down a peg.

SOURCE: Retold with permission from "The Hungry Fox and the Boastful Suitor" in *Iroquois Stories: Heroes and Heroines, Monsters and Magic* by Joseph Bruchac, © 1985 The Crossing Press: Freedom, CA. Also on the Internet http://www.indians.org/weller/natlit. htm.

The Tortoise Who Rode an Elephant

In this Yoruba story from Nigeria, it is Tortoise's pride and boastfulness— and a touch of greed too—that drive him to trick Elephant.

SOURCE: Retold with permission from "How Tortoise Rode Elephant to Town" in *King Leopard's Gift and Other Legends of the Animal World* by Rosalind Kerven (Cambridge University Press, 1990).

The Very Clever Rabbit

This was told to my friend Maria Thomas (née Cabello) when she was a little girl in Caracas, by her Venezuelan grandmother, Josefina Alvarez. I have added details, such as the gender of the rabbit and the dialogue.

The Animal Who Couldn't Make Up Its Mind

"Poor platypus could not make up his mind what he wanted, and ended up with the parts of many animals." So said the version of the Australian creation myth I read, and it inspired me to write the story behind those words.

SOURCE: "The Strange Shape of Animals" in *Myths and Legends of Australia* by A.W. Reed (A.H. & A.W. Reed, Australia, 1965).

Every effort has been made to trace and contact copyright holders before publication. If any errors or omissions have occurred, Frances Lincoln Limited will be pleased to rectify these at the earliest opportunity.